Help me
carry the stone

Help me carry the stone

Sean Aramesh

Library of Congress Control Number: 2020922879
ISBN: Hardcover   978-1-6641-4286-2
                      Softcover   978-1-6641-4285-5
                      eBook   978-1-6641-4284-8

Print information available on the last page.

Rev. date: 11/13/2020

To order additional copies of this book, contact:
Xlibris
844-714-8691
www.Xlibris.com
Orders@Xlibris.com
821202

For those who love

rivers, streams

and aliens

For

Maziar

Mandana

Dice

Shaza

Nadya

Rameen

and the cat

Einstein

for the spiritual guidance and support given by

Tatum

Chapter 1

Once there were two species on a distant planet. No more than one of each species existed; they were the only ones of their kind. But there was one problem. On that planet, there was a lack of resources for living, and finding natural food was nearly impossible. Therefore, it was a struggle to survive.

The planet itself was surrounded by stars, moons, and other planets in the galaxy. Were they alone? Were the two species the only two beings that existed in the entire universe? Well, we are yet to find out.

Their planet had a view of bright colors scattered across space, with trillions of stars that make up simple galaxies. The two exotic creatures, being highly intelligent, were, no doubt, already studying philosophy in their own minds.

Although we are at the point of the story where these two have not yet met, they both already have a strong mental connection with each other. It was as though some sort of energy field existed between them, and it would eventually lead them to meeting each other.

Philosophy was the main thing on their minds. They wondered where they came from, the nature of the bright colors of the night sky, the planets, the moons, and the colorful stars. They both pondered one strange curiosity: What is out there in the universe? But though these two miraculous beings have so much in common, they both dreaded the day when they will finally have to meet each other.

Why should they dread meeting each other? They have so much in common. They are both highly intelligent, they think about the same things, and most of all, loneliness has taken a toll on both of them.

It was because they knew there would be a fight for personal space. They would also probably have to fight for resources to live on a planet that was covered mostly with large craters full of rainwater.

The stars were close to the planet, and the light they made reflected on the moons, causing moonlight. There was no sun, so it seemed as though it was nighttime all the time. But the stars were colorful and shined brightly along with the moon.

The description of the two beings that lived there made them easy to imagine. They both had regular arms and legs, with regular heads and torsos. They had fingers and toes just like us. One of them had skin that would glow and change colors with the stars. The being seemed to always have the same facial expression, as if he was always calm and perfectly at peace. But occasionally, he would smile with such a great emotion. This being had so much personality.

The other being represented physical strength. He was strong, and his senses were powerful. He was also highly aware that he was not alone on this planet. His skin was almost transparent, making it look like the black ink outline of a black-and-white comic book. He was a lot bigger and had more muscle mass compared with the other one.

They both could go for years without food or even sleep. Being on opposite sides of the planet, they knew nothing of kindness, caring, giving, or sharing a life with someone they could call a friend.

It was always quiet in their planet. Sometimes they could hear the quiet sounds of planetary shifts from underneath the ground, but it was always peaceful. Sometimes there were soft sounds coming through the atmosphere. Nice quiet sounds would flow through the air, like something out of a Pink Floyd song or maybe slow drops of water dripping from large stones. But for the most part, the planet was usually completely silent, dark too for there was no sun, only the slight brightness of the stars. The ground was dry and hard like rough limestone. Dark gray rocky ground covered the whole planet, with tiny holes going through it, similar to limestone that filters water. Some parts of the planet was made of something like hard black volcanic rock but shiny like black glass. So as you can see, the planet was a combination of bright colors from the sky, peaceful calmness from the natural sounds in the air, and relaxing darkness with no sun.

As I said before, there were large craters filled with rainwater. These craters were large enough to hold enough water to make a small lake or a natural spring to relax in.

Imagine the privacy you would have there. The freedom to do what you want and have everything you need. You would be bothered by no one, with no other living thing on your own personal planet. No fish to ruin your swim. No plants, no birds even. There were only the soft sounds to reach your ears, and the only view is of either the natural darkness on the ground or colorful skies. It is a beautiful private planet where you can peacefully live out your days and die with no sadness.

Would you get lonely? Would you dread a life of having everything to yourself? Would you get bored? Imagine yourself there, at peace and in tune with all of existence. No religion. No belief of any kind. No one to force any kind of teachings upon you, such as education, hard work, what to do, and what not to do. No one to invade your privacy. Would this be called freedom? Or would it be just a sense of being trapped, imprisoned in a life that leads nowhere? It would be a deserted planet where you have no motivation to migrate and see if anyone else exists. Would you feel trapped with all this intelligence, always wondering if there might be something out there when you look at the night sky? Would you start a fire out of boredom? Or would you seek technology to leave the planet?

So many thoughts and possibilities may come to your mind. Your emotions may get in the way of any plans you make for the future. Would you express your emotions by writing them down? Would you let out your feelings out in an artistic way? Would you become your own scientist or artist? If you had a whole planet to yourself, there would be no end to the possibilities. But the sad part is you would still have restrictions and limitations. If you do not have the natural ability to fly, then you would have to figure it out yourself (if that was your dream).

All people today face these issues, and it seems as though you can never run away from your problems. Here on Earth, we are surrounded by people, plants, animals, schools, jobs, sickness, mental illness, and many more things that are always in our way. It is as if our privacy is always completely invaded. But if we had an entire galaxy to ourselves and were alone on a planet that we cannot leave without the proper technology, would we still suffer just as much? That is the biggest mystery of them all, the curious question that runs through the minds of every living species in the universe.

Would we be better off alone with no one to bother us? There would be nothing to make us fight for survival. Nothing to make us need health care, money, success, or all the desires for luxury. A planet with no crime. No need for weapons to feel threatened by. No invisible divine being who brings difficulty and anger into our hearts. No religion, not even atheism or belief in reincarnation.

For me, these are the aspects of life that we cannot escape. We can feel free but never be truly free, it seems. Frustration is something we cannot escape. Therefore, we all eventually become the madmen of the universe. These are the facts that we face our entire lives.

Some people try to send positive messages through motivational speeches or kind words, such as "Believe in yourself, you are wonderful, you got this, don't give up." But these are just words to help us through hardships, and no actual hope is ever given to us in life. We never come out of it; we never get what we are promised. Instead, we keep on fighting to get true happiness, which does not even exist.

Now back to the two beings on the deserted planet. The advantages they had are beyond us. They were extremely intelligent beings who lived and died long before I began telling this story.

Before even meeting, they both already sensed that they were not alone. Each wanted the planet to himself, and because of this, they hated each other and became worst enemies. They were like rivals in a private world, two private beings who preferred to be alone and to not deal with someone else trying to take over what is theirs.

As one of them enjoyed a natural hot spring by the place he lived in, the other one was on the other side of the planet, lifting rocks to make shelter for himself. But it was inevitable that they would meet one day.

What do you say to a person who has no choice? Could you comfort them? Could you make sure they are okay? Or can you just tell them that they are going to be okay? No words can assure a person about his future in life. Will two people with no direction find it with each other? Or will they rather find direction without each other? Should they meet and become two enemies who learn to live together in peace? Two rivals can become close and learn to respect each other in order to survive. They could put aside their differences, live together in harmony, and become friends who would die to protect each other. Two good, honest beings lived on that planet, but they hated each other before they even met, only later realizing that they need each other to not stay lonely.

Could these two enemies come together with compassion and understand the importance of friendship? Love would make a promise for death to make an angel of a person, to die for a close friend. Love and poetry go hand in hand. Hold hands with your loved one, the one whom you would sacrifice your soul for, just like two people alone on a planet waiting for the sun to brighten the darkness even though the sun will never come. The moon will break apart as life starts to deteriorate.

Maybe the Earth's moon is not meant to last for very long. I believe that the moon will slowly break apart into pieces as life begins to go extinct.

I write this story while the world is being quarantined. It seems as though the virus has become unstoppable; the world has become a slave to the end of humankind. There seems to be hope, but we fight this virus with no vaccine, no leads, and no trace of a cure to save humans from inevitable destruction. Has this become a problem even though fate is unavoidable anyway?

I believe we should start thinking about the aftermath of life instead of how to temporarily fight for survival. What will give people on Earth assurance of peace? Maybe nobody knows. But let us not give up only because of fate. Otherwise, what are we doing all this for?

Most people stay motivated to exercise and eat right, to work on keeping our health up. What do we work so hard for? Is it for good deeds, such as helping others and staying motivated? Let's not let it lead us nowhere, as if fate makes all our efforts pointless, with "fate" being our expiration date.

Let us get back. As the one with gentleness and a calm expression on his face stands on a small hill and looks down into the water to see his reflection, the other looks at the shelter he had spent hours making, enjoying his creation. Pride and joy cause him to want to add beauty to his new home. But unfortunately, his home seems to need the touch of another living being. Therefore, friendship is on his mind.

Now back to the other one. He slowly steps into his reflection and enjoys the beauty of his own personal Jacuzzi. He finds peace in his mind knowing that he has a choice between being alone or having a friend to show his stuff to.

Let us not let negativity get in the way. Instead, let us follow a life of passion. Positivity will give us security, so let us go toward that. If we make the right decisions in life that lead toward pleasant feelings, we can live together in friendship, just like these two can.

Life revolves around choice, just as a miracle relies purely on choice. A teenager who says "no" to drugs and "yes" to an education is a miracle. Our choices can change our destinies; they can shift our futures. Good choices can mold our minds and cause us to have a better life. Going for a run instead of sleeping the day away or having a piece of fruit instead of a piece of chocolate for a snack can help increase our lifespan. A man or a woman getting up every day to go to work instead of accepting dishonest money is a miracle, but it is also because of a choice. Just like worst enemies becoming best friends, which is also a choice.

Here now is a more in-depth view of this deep science fiction story, based on life and how we choose to live it. Within the last two million years, mankind has faced many challenges. A lot of these challenges involved anger and prejudice. Religious conflicts are still a part of human challenges on Earth to this day. Emotions can become stable if we set aside the way we see one another, such as how we see the color of our skin. People come from different walks of life. Regardless of where we are from, what matters is what we can learn from one another if we open up our hearts and just listen. Some of us might not have much to say, but we will eventually start to open up if we trust the people around us. Every person has the ability to love and have compassion. But as mentioned before, choice has a lot to do with direction.

As you can see, unlike every other science fiction story, no use of advanced technology has taken place so far. Instead, I have used creative landscapes and skies that are full of beautiful stars, with two noble people of a different species who are in tune with their surroundings, as a Zen master would be in a deep state of meditation. But in this case, everything is happening on a distant planet.

You can also take in the wisdom of my personal experiences through my own journey in life. The being that I mentioned had physical strength was very much into expressing the truth, which was his own beliefs of right and wrong. He believed in following an honest path in life and being an honest person. He also believed in appreciating what life had provided for him. His beliefs were what he lived his life by, such as respecting the stars, the moons, and the solar system. He respected the beauty of his abilities, knowing that he was blessed with everything he had and believing that he should be grateful for all of it. He was a particularly good person with honest beliefs.

The other, as I said before, was always so peaceful and had a relaxing life. He always had a calm expression on his face. But he did not have any beliefs or loyalty toward anything. But he was very much in tune with his surroundings. He loved connecting with the galaxy. He was a meditator, a loving being who appreciated nature. Both were very kind people, definitely people you would want to make friends with.

Neither of them had parents. They both evolved and developed from the elements of the planet. Their bodies were made up of the same ingredients that the planet was made up of.

It is the same with us here on Earth. For example, if you were to look at the ingredients in a multivitamin, you would find iron, magnesium, copper, zinc, and selenium, which are found in soil; chromium, which is used to make chrome; hydrogen, oxygen, carbon, and nitrogen, which are found in the Earth's atmosphere; and many more natural elements that the Earth is made up of. We come from the Earth, and therefore, we are made up of the Earth's main elements.

On an alien planet, where life has also come from the ground and atmosphere, whatever living on it is made up of the elements in that world as well. This concept can be understood through either creationism or evolutionism.

At this point, they have both experienced something new, a fresh scent in the air. Even while on opposite sides of the planet, they could smell each other. Of course, each had their own smell, but both were like a fragrant perfume made from the most beautiful scent in the galaxy. Both quickly turned their heads and began to take in the sweet scent. Their natural scent was more fragrant than any smell you and I have ever smelled. They smelled like a combination of rare flowers and lovely essential oils, and it was even nicer than the smell of the most high-quality perfume in existence. They finally had some form of contact with each other.

Some say that smell is the sense that is most strongly tied to memory; therefore, it is a fact that they will never forget this experience. But even their smell did not make them want to meet, for they loved their privacy, and both would still fight to defend it. Even though they could smell each other (that beautiful smell!), each still wanted the planet to himself. Therefore, they remained archenemies.

Could we possibly imagine the favors that life would bring them if these two came together in friendship? Each of them would have someone to care for, and have someone care for them. They would get each other through loneliness and boredom. Share knowledge to maybe create artistic hobbies. Use their intelligence to perhaps leave the planet and explore the rest of the solar system.

They could start with making fires together and bonding with each other, then move to inventing highly-advanced technology. They might find that they have so much in common and eventually develop a society if they find other aliens in the rest of the galaxy.

With so much to look at with the stars, moons, and other planets in the sky, there is no end to the possibilities.

By now, these two have reached the age of a full-grown adult. With no sun, they have adapted to darkness. This might be the reason they are always at peace.

Think about when we sleep at night. It is dark out, and we turn off the lights so that we can sleep. That is because our eyes need that darkness, and that natural darkness is what we need in order to rest and grow. It relaxes us so that we can sleep and rejuvenate.

The same goes on their planet. Since they do not have a sun, it is always dark. This keeps them in a calm and peaceful state all the time. But unlike Earth, they have brighter stars very close to their planet, making them still able to see. Therefore, they can go for years without sleep. Also, they have adapted to the lack of abundance of food on the planet and can go for long periods with no food.

It does not seem too boring, just too quiet. The air makes soft sounds, sounds you can almost see. There is no wind, just a soothing sound that comes and goes with neon-colored visuals, as if you could see the slow but beautiful sounds.

Chapter 2

A person would be convinced to not fear anything in a world like theirs. Nothing but kindness seems to exist there. The universe is kind to them and gives them what life should give a person.

So it seems that these two owe life a little kindness in return. They both know that they can share. They both know and feel what is right and wrong. The two incredibly special people owe it to the gifts of the galaxy to add love and care to their lives. They both know there is someone to share their life with. These two are now ready to meet.

For the first time, each of them begins to travel across the planet. They have a strong mental connection with each other; they know that if they get up and start walking now, they can meet halfway.

After a short travel across an enormous planet, they finally see each other. As they walk up to meet the other, they notice the exhaustion and relaxation in each other's eyes. They look each other in the eyes and notice so many emotions, such as excitement, happiness, and relief; of course, they also see a smile on each other's faces.

They have anticipated this moment for so long. And they owe it to themselves for being patient. Life has brought them nothing but gifts, and now it has brought them friendship. It was always destiny that they would come together as friends and not enemies, having both lived such an honest life, taking care of their health and respecting their planet.

All that matters now is that they have relief and quite possibly an amazing journey ahead of them.

Together, they walk north to the top of the highest hill at the top of their world. There is no need to develop speech, for they understood each other so well. They now were in a constant state of bonding with each other. As they walked, they could hear each other's quiet vibrations coming from deep within their souls. Their faces were bright and full of joy.

They make it to the top and stop to see something mysterious on the ground. It was a small circle filled with lava. They both had amazing instincts, so they sit across each other with the lava between them, as if they were sitting around a campfire. They begin to touch and feel the lava. It was not hot and had a nice texture. As they touched it, they got the same sensation that a child would get from playing with slime for the first time.

This wonderful discovery they had made was of a natural substance underneath the ground. They are soon to discover that this natural substance will be the beginning of technology for them. It meant that they can create a new world with it and even find ways to travel in space.

As they examined it, they looked up at each other and smiled with excitement. There could be so much more wonderful things hidden on the planet.

In the meantime, one of them (the strong one) wanted to show the other the shelter that he had built. He made a hand gesture as if to say, "Follow me." He brought him to his living area with great hospitality. It was a cozy shelter he had made, but as I mentioned before, it needed decoration. That is why he brought him here. It was a big home made only from large stones that only a person of great physical strength could carry. But it had no colors, except for that of the gray limestone-like ground there.

So the other being began to make this shelter look like a home. He used his ability to make his skin glow to add bright neon colors to the roof and walls. He even added a red door and a chandelier inside.

They spent the next many hours sitting side by side, bonding with each other as they stared up at the sky. How wonderful that these two came together and became such good friends.

Then they both went inside for a long nap. The home was large enough for ten or more people to fit comfortably inside.

The natural substance they had found up north was always in the back of their minds. They wondered what it might be and why it was there. It seemed to be another gift that life had given them, a favor in return of a favor for all their honest decisions.

They spend many months on this side of the planet, living in harmony with each other. They share their memories and relax peacefully together. They are remarkably simple and happy people. But what now? What comes next?

The love that these two share as friends would only grow stronger until the day they pass on. They could not stop dreaming of exploring and seeing what could exist in the rest of the galaxy. The meditator then had an idea to travel up north to experiment with the lava-like substance. When they reached the top of the highest hill, they knelt to pull some of it out with their hands.

Teleportation was the only thing they could think of. How could they use a natural source without any kind of machinery to teleport to a distant star or a moon somewhere? It is simple.

What do we know so far about these two aliens and their world? We know they both live with peace and within nature. They are one with the universe. They are extremely intelligent. And most of all, they are dreamers.

Dreamers are the ones who make flying machines, such as airplanes and space rockets. Dreamers are the ones like you (the reader) who believe in alternate universes and alien beings, people who know that there is more to life that just chemistry and science. A dreamer is someone like you who choose to keep reading this story and have faith in beauty, motivation, and honesty. I appreciate you for believing and staying motivated to make it this far. And for that, I thank you.

No more time to waste. Let us teleport. This natural chemical substance does not have a name. The characters in the story do not have a name. Neither does the planet, the moons, or the galaxy they live in. Thus far, they have never thought of giving names to themselves or anything else. Names are something that seems required in a society full of other people, places, and things.

So far, there is no need to name anything, except for the natural substance. They have not developed any form of speech and, therefore, can only communicate through the power of the mind. For the first time, they finally develop the power of speech and use it to say a phrase: "the gift."

Their voices were unbelievably phenomenal. Voices that you could spend hours listening to. There was more power in their voices than any beautiful piece of music you and I have ever heard.

They took their eyes off each other and looked down again. They had named their discovery "the gift." They felt as if life had given them something so miraculous and important. They valued and cherished "the gift" almost as much as they valued their friendship. But their friendship will always remain the most important thing in their lives until the day they come to pass.

For some reason, they dreamed of the moon closest to them, and together, they teleported there. When they arrived at the moon, they noticed nothing but what they expected to see. It was gray, rocky, dusty, and empty. Not quite different from our moon, quiet and empty.

They knew there had to be something farther out there worth seeing, something among the faraway stars and the colors that they always saw when they looked up. From there, they decided to go somewhere more reasonable, a planet, one extremely far from their current location.

Being on another planet was beyond them. It was always something they thought they would never experience.

Chapter 3

They were slowly developing more words. "Let's go there," they said, and there they were. They were so used to living on a planet with dark gray rocky ground, black volcanic glass, and small craters filled water. They were tired of that same scenery.

This planet they just teleported to was mostly thick blue ground. The ground was full of land, which was like thick blue marmalade, hard enough to walk on. They sense something special was there. Life. They knew there was life on other planets, and they knew they found a planet where they can find other beings.

They walked around. The sky looked like pink cotton candy. What a trippy place. But still, no signs of life.

As they walked, they finally saw someone. And then there were more people. There were beings remarkably similar to them. They looked and acted so friendly. Of course, they had not developed the power of speech yet. It was a small group of people living peacefully together.

As I come to this part of the story, I am reminded of my childhood. It is like walking up to a group of people at the basketball court or the skate park to hang out with other skaters, making friends with people who seemed decent enough. I am sure many can relate to looking for people to socialize with. It is as simple as it sounds. You're young, you see some other kids hanging out, and you just go over and talk to them. Friendship is important, as far as I know. You should never let go of your friends. Introducing one to another creates new friendships. As long as you believe in yourself and you trust your decisions, making new friends should be pretty easy. Let me demonstrate.

They simply walked over to the group of people. These new beings they had found were very hospitable. They invited them right into their group of friends. Why not? The more, the merrier. They were aliens treating other aliens like valuable individuals. They were in a new beautiful brightly-colored planet with a loving atmosphere and good people just like you and me. It doesn't get much better than this.

They lived together for months. Time passed slowly, but things progressed. They developed new ways to live and pass the time. They shared stories of their past and created new memories, living together in harmony. What a wonderful group of people. What a nice time they had together for almost a year now on this beautiful new planet. It was sort of like a society that they had developed with the beings they met.

Finally, they began to think of other planets that may have life on them. They shared their knowledge of teleportation with their new friends and the natural substance they called "the gift." They brought them all to the planet where they lived in when they met each other and showed them "the gift." When the crowd of people looked at it, their eyes lit up. To them, it was the most fantastic thing they had ever seen. They dipped their hands in it to examine its texture. Their hands began to glow. They never felt anything like it. They all decided to teleport together to other places, and they went to the stars nearby.

Stars, as we know it, are made up of gas and other chemicals that make them shine brightly. Some scientists here on Earth believe that each star exists like the sun, with planets around it, just like in the Milky Way galaxy.

The aliens, of course, were not burned by the stars they were standing on. It felt like a science experiment to them, seeing how bright the stars were and how they were able to give light. Of course, these stars were small, nothing like the size of the sun. Perhaps they could find a way to bring the stars together to make something bright enough to light up every planet. That way, it would not seem like it was nighttime all the time.

This was their new idea: They wanted to build a sun.

The idea would be greatly beneficial to the entire solar system. As you know, they do not have a sun to brighten up the planets, just stars to make a little bit of light. Therefore, if they build a sun for the galaxy, it will no longer seem like it was nighttime all the time.

Have you ever heard the saying, "If you want something bad enough, you can accomplish it"? It is like the man who invented the first automobile or a child who dreams of being an astronaut when he grows up. These things take guts, and sometimes guts are enough if you want something badly enough. Just like how a group of alien beings wanted to build a sun in their distant solar system are able to do it because they are dreamers.

About a thousand gallons of "the gift" and a thousand stars should have enough energy to brighten the planets. It is as if magic was involved in their dream of building a sun. They just wished for it, and suddenly, for the first time ever, it was daytime on their planet.

Everything looked so bright. It was such a beautiful day. The new sun was shining, and they could see one another's faces so clearly. It was a brand-new world for them. They could see the true color of the ground, which was no longer gray and black.

Over the next few days, seedlings began to sprout into green grass. The sky lightly rained down, and flowers and plant life existed for the first time. The sky was blue with clouds.

They built a shelter, a beautiful home. They had bright sunny days, plants, grass, sunsets, and sunrises. It was a spectacular planet full of fruits and fresh water. The simple yet brilliant idea of building a sun had changed their lives forever.

Our two main characters, as you know, were men. But among the group, there were separate genders for them to procreate and slowly build a society.

All this was going on simply because two people decided to set their differences aside and become friends.

The importance of love is deep within our hearts. We all know the value of kindness. Life is a little messed up sometimes, but we all have value. And if we reach deep down inside, we can all find what matters most: love.

Love, kindness, and caring—these created a new existence so important that it would last forever.

If aliens in a distant galaxy were able to find the true meaning behind life, maybe we can too.

"The gift." By now, this natural technology has given them two abilities. The first one was teleportation, and then they used it to bring a thousand stars together to build a sun. What else could they use it for? Many years have passed. The aliens have grown from a small society to a large one. They have made new worlds on different planets. They kept reproducing and even kept finding more life-forms on new planets. They all lived together in harmony within one galaxy. They mostly communicated through power of the mind, but they still use the power of speech from time to time.

They were still a very peaceful people, a large population of alien beings living across one large galaxy. There was so much going on, and "the gift" has brought them so many incredible amounts of beauty. It has made them stronger, friendlier, calmer, and more peaceful. Years have gone by, and trillions of aliens lived together in perfect harmony.

Only a small handful of people knew the two beings who had started all this. They did not care too much for publicity. They just wanted to live their lives and not brag about their decision of becoming friends, which caused a chain reaction of such magnitude.

Chapter 4

Time passed, as time does. The two beings have grown older. They do not boast about themselves, although they know that they are the only ones who really matter in this story. They only wish the best for everyone, and they continue to treat each other well as the years go by.

Thank you for keeping up thus far.

As you remember, the stronger one had beliefs about existence and appreciating the gift of life in every sense of the word. He was a believer, like one who was in a religion. His life revolved around thanking the world he came from, as if he was praying to a form of creation. This is the reason they both remained on their original planet to live out their lives. He believed in the truth that he came from the ground and he will one day die and be buried in the ground. He was a great man.

As you also remember the other one who was in tune with his surroundings, he was also an incredibly good person, but he had never given thought to appreciating life or anything it had given him. He was a very respectful man with kindness and hospitality, and he was very much a gentleman. But he wanted to learn of the path and beliefs that his lifelong friend lived by.

He had been studying him and his ways since the beginning. He has seen him pray, how much he valued his beliefs, and what a good person it made him. He was very inspired by his way of life. Eventually, he began to ask him about it, using their speech.

"You are very appreciative of life's gifts," he said.

"Yes," the other replied. "I believe in many things other than just living in peace."

This grabbed his attention. "What else is there other than living in peace?"

The other's reply would remain in his memory until the day he died. "We are the chosen people. We were put here for a reason. One day we will die, and then the actions we made during our time here will be all that is left of our existence. If we do not thank life for everything it has given us, then that makes us worthless. In the beginning, we had such anger toward each other. But belief is what made me change my mind. You see, we must give to the people that give us love and a good life. If we do not return the favor of life, then we will not reap its benefits. In other words, we must live for a greater reason than ourselves."

These are the same concepts taught to us in life. If we choose to accept goodness and kindness, then we will receive more in return.

From then on, he became both his teacher and his student. He taught him the ways of gratefulness. He taught him the reason that we give to instead of take away from one another. He went on to explain his beliefs. He taught him truth. He explained the reason he prays.

"This is to give thanks to what we have experienced together as lifelong friends, the power of change, love, kindness and giving. Therefore, I pray."

This was fascinating for the other one to hear and learn about. He did not think that his friend's beliefs were wrong. He wanted to learn all that he could from his beliefs. This brought them even closer together.

It was a deep friendship that they had. They were bonding with each other in ways that are unimaginable to us.

Hearing more about his beliefs, he eventually said, "I have felt and experienced all this before and even before we met."

"Of course, you have. Truth is truth, and it cannot be changed. Truth has always existed, and it always will exist. We cannot change the power of truth. Therefore, if we accept it, we can lead a life of harmony."

And this is what they have done together. They met and led a life of harmony from a single quiet planet to an entire galaxy of other beings, living and reflecting off the peaceful nature that these two had. Without knowing it, they had lived a life of purity and goodness. They built a sun together. They met other aliens and became friends with them. They never made enemies in the entire universe. The galaxy procreated, and only peaceful beings came into existence one after another. It was simply because these two miraculous people came together in friendship and never let greed get between them.

Drawing and writing things down became a new hobby. They started writing stories together about all their experiences. They would draw pictures to go along with the stories, as if they were writing an autobiography.

From this, they eventually started writing the first books in existence, starting with an autobiography with both of their names were written on the cover. It was the story of their journey through life, along with sketches to express their artistic side. Using the magic of "the gift," they were able to put paper together in the form of books. They started writing fictional stories about time travel or whatever else came to their minds. The power they felt while holding a book in their hands motivated them to keep writing.

They began distributing their books to the people. Everyone enjoyed reading and getting lost in the stories within the magical pages. They spent their time writing and relaxing. They wrote about science, belief, history, and made many novels.

Science. They wrote about history and the beginning of time, how they evolved from the universe, and how all are made of the elements of the universe.

Belief. They wrote about truth and what the strong one spoke about, the purpose of life, and how they need to appreciate the gifts of life.

History. They wrote about before they built the sun, how they discovered "the gift" and how it changed history. They wrote about meeting other people by teleportation and how society grew from a small group of friends to trillions of aliens living across their entire galaxy.

Novels. Fiction. Stories that would take the reader to another place. Tales of dragons and flying machines, romance, and peace. Whatever they could think of that would interest their friends and encourage them to read.

More artistic talents began to develop from their hearts. They began to make music and sing about their emotions. They would play their music for the people, deep songs about life. Their lyrics were phenomenal and unique.

Painting became a new kind of art. They would draw and paint detailed pictures of the night sky. They would paint portraits, scenery, flowers, trees, and anything an intelligent artist could think of.

In this galaxy lived trillions of aliens. Everybody did what they wanted. There was no crime, no fighting in any way. People shared and learned about one another. Everyone helped one another. The power of kindness will always keep them safe from any harm.

Most days the two would lay around bonding. The bond they had continued to grow deeper within their hearts. It became their favorite thing to do.

Letting time pass was the most important thing. They lived their lives slowly because time passed slowly.

As we study the Milky Way, there is so much to be seen. Mars is a planet that has always fascinated us, with its orange glow and the mystery behind what might be there or even the fact that life might have existed there at one point. We are yet to still set foot on the planet Mars; only machines have made it there so far. It is still too dangerous for a person to visit the planet. At least we are doing the best we can.

Nine planets have been found in the Milky Way, Pluto being the farthest. If we were to travel that far, we would be too far from the sun, and therefore, we would have to visit Pluto with extreme caution. It would be too cold there. We would have to make sure that we can stay warm.

Stars are farther away than any planet in the night sky. Will we one day get light years away from Earth, far enough to reach the galaxy where the two beings in the story live? Would they welcome us there? Would we be a part of their lives? I say, of course. Their hospitality is important to them. We would learn a life with no conflict, just like theirs. We would feed off their energy. We would share our history and listen to theirs.

Even though this is a science fiction story, we might be able to find them one day.

And let us say we did. Our dreams can one day become realities if we dream hard enough. Does it all have to be fiction? What would be the reason for listening to their story? It is for remembering them. Nobody knows if the stories in our own history are true. The evolution of man, apes to humans, fossil remains—these are all we have to recreate the past in the best way we can. Are the stories and legends about Zeus and the Greek gods true?

Will *Help Me Carry the Stone* become a legend of its own someday? Or will it be just another book thrown on a shelf somewhere? Either way, I will not get my feelings hurt.

Everything perishes in some way or another. I think it is beautiful.

Just like how our two favorite characters will eventually perish and turn to dust, to be forgotten in time as if they never lived. People in their galaxy will live on for the rest of time, but will these two be remembered? I guarantee you they will not. Do you keep up with the people you went to kindergarten with? Or the people you met at your first job? Do you even remember them? Our two main characters will be gone just like we eventually will be. I think it is beautiful. Will you remember me? Will I ever meet you?

People—individuals, personalities, and their lifestyles—are another main part of this story. Our past and where we are from will vanish and disappear and be nothing but a mess to be swept away by a broom.

Chapter 5

As our two main characters sit like gargoyles inside their home, more aliens are colonizing other planets. Their society is growing at an increasing rate. Their planet has now flourished with waterfalls, trees, and strange new animals. No more dark craters filled with rainwater. No more hard, gray, limestone-like ground. No more darkness or loneliness, like it was before they built a sun.

But what now? What comes next? They are simply passing the time. They have learned about each other's beliefs. They have already bonded to the maximum limit. It is time for these two to think up a way to have real fun.

Rituals, as we know, are the regular ways that we as people do things naturally. There are also social gatherings, which would be a great idea, something they could look forward to. It may need more than two heads to come up with some new ideas.

You are never too old to make new friends. They finally started coming out of their house every day, mostly going for walks, saying "Hello" to the people passing by. They began seeing other homes, meeting aliens, both male and female, living all around their planet.

People of all ages—children, teenagers, parents, families, and friends—all became happy. They never realized that they were not really doing much every day. Our two characters were now in their middle ages. They went over and spoke to a couple with children.

"Anything new going on the planet lately?"

"The same as usual. Our children are happy, and that is enough for us." They simply smiled and continued to walk.

They needed new friends. A wonderful new idea then shined upon them.

In Erich von Däniken's 1968 classic *Chariots of the Gods*, the author speaks about visitors arriving on Earth in flying machines during the days of the ancient pyramids. He refers to many ancient artifacts that were designed with pictures of aliens carved into them. The book mentions so much incredible evidence of alien beings visiting Earth thousands of years ago. Please consider researching these marvelous discoveries for yourself. There is much information recorded about it.

As you know, this story took place long ago.

However, they have been walking and meeting new people every day around the planet. After communicating with most of their neighbors, they realized how much ability and skill each alien had. They were normal people, nice people, mostly people with families. But they had one thing in common: They had *talent*. Imagine what they can do with that talent.

As I mentioned earlier, our ancient pyramids may have been made by visitors from another planet. It is not officially known how the pyramids were made. Each brick weighs over two tons, which is the weight of almost two cars. The only guess we have is that they could have used rollers made of wood to push the bricks. But the few brittle trees that grew near the ancient pyramids could not have withstood the weight of each brick. No logical explanation have been made about how those bricks were stacked on top of one another by human beings. It couldn't have been done. Even with the resources we have today, we still would not be able to build pyramids like the ones in Egypt.

Our two main characters had made a decision. They wanted to build pyramids.

The reason they had was to have something for people to gather around every day and to simply have something to do. At the same time, it could be a form of a social gathering they could look forward to. They could hang out and meet new people, find friends, and make new hobbies. They would also be making something they could be proud of by building a pyramid.

With the magical help of "the gift," they found a way to make this dream become a reality.

They spread the word of the exciting new idea. It was like having a fair in a small town for people to come together for enjoyment. Our two favorite aliens brought as many gallons of "the gift" as possible.

All the local aliens came at sunset to gather and meet new people. They had never seen a huge pond full of "the gift" before, and this excited them. They started building fires and socializing with one another, watching the sun slowly go down. At least now people can meet one another.

They spoke about the idea of the pyramids with everyone. They explained that building a pyramid had no real purpose but to bring people together as one. It is a simple thing to make, just a triangular monument.

It was just something for them to gather around every night, so they could hang out and have something to do. It was a unanimous decision among all them, of course. They had complex yet simple minds.

Friendship. They focused everyone's mind toward friendship and images of children playing together, teenagers finding dates, and grown-ups sharing their memories with one another. It was a new era, and it was the beginning of a new way of life for aliens as they knew it.

Weeks fell off the calendar as the enormous pyramid was being built. More and more aliens came from the planets nearby to watch it grow. Luckily, they have not gotten bored of it yet.

Word spread around the galaxy about the triangular monument being made, and more groups of aliens from far away come to watch it being built. Some of them even join in and begin to help.

Not once did any one of them wonder who the masterminds behind this idea were.

Luckily for us, we know them personally.

Exhaustion. Our two favorite friends have never been this exhausted in their lives. As I mentioned before, they could go for months or even years without sleep. After all, that has been going on for the past few years. The two went home and simply passed out.

They slept like bears hibernating during winter, going into a deep sleep. They felt so cozy and relaxed. They spent months sleeping away ages of effort and dedication. The tiredness on the bottom of their feet went away. Their minds took a long break. Their body and soul rested, sleeping away all the exhaustion they had.

Months went by, and they continued to sleep like babies. They dreamed of clouds and exotic animals, dreams that took them far away and made them forget how tired they were.

Eventually, they woke. When they opened their eyes, it was as if they were in another world. They were so rested. Happy to be awake, they spent hours stretching and yawning. With their eyes barely opened, they slowly walked out of their house. Still yawning, stretching, and scratching themselves, they slowly walked to the river, which was just a few feet away from their front door. They used their hands to splash some fresh water on their faces and began to open their eyes wider.

How refreshing, after months of deep sleep. What a feeling! Now completely rested, stretching had never felt so good.

They looked at each other and began to laugh. They felt silly, but they gave each other a great hug to say hello.

Now, of course, much had changed over a period of many months. They looked around, still sitting by the river. They looked up at the sun. It was so bright and beautiful. It was such a nice day. The temperature in the air was just right, not too cold and not too hot. There were so many more trees and bright green plants. They could think of nothing but to sit by the river and watch the water flow.

"How long do you think we have been out?"

"A few days, I think," the strong one replied.

After many hours of sitting in silence by the river, they both walked back inside. They cooked and had some fresh food and water.

Coming from the window, they noticed the sun was brighter than usual, so they went outside to look. The pyramid was finished, and it was glowing a bright orange. It was the most fantastic thing they had ever seen.

The pyramid was so enormous and covered with multiple coats of "the gift," which was making it shine brightly. It was a glowing large triangular phenomenon! And people were still standing on top of it, covering it with gallons and gallons of "the gift."

People were laughing and talking, hanging out next to the pyramid and having a great time.

Now back to what I was saying about our ancient pyramids in Egypt. The aliens had no problem building one the size of the ones we have here. However, it would have taken many generations and many lifetimes for humans to build even just one here on Earth (considering the size of them and the fact that each brick weighs two and a half tons). So how was it done?

As I mentioned earlier, some museums have ancient artifacts with pictures of flying machines carved on them. And a lot of ancient ruins tell stories of visitors from the sky coming to Earth thousands of years ago.

Could it be that our pyramids were built long ago by visitors from this alien galaxy? The one in our story?

Could it be a simple coincidence that you are reading this story now? This story of science fiction, key word being *fiction*. *Help Me Carry the Stone* is in the fiction section.

Even *Schindler's List* is in the fiction section.

Please look through *The Confederation of American Natives*, where I relate alien contact with my personal studies and understanding of the third eye.

Perhaps all things in the history of the universe are "fact" or "fiction" in one way or another.

Back to the story. Could it be that the effort these two gave since the beginning somehow resulted in creating one of the most historical memories in the pages of history? To me, it seems that giving an honest effort toward a dream that you have will make that dream possible. Setting goals and going toward your vision of yourself will also determine where you will be in the future. These two had a dream, and they made it happen. In fact, they have reached several goals in their life up until now.

Chapter 6

Inside the shelter, both of them were sitting like Buddhists. One day it began to rain. The clouds overhead got dark and began to cover the sky. The glow from the pyramid stayed bright. They lit the candles in their home and the torches outside by the front door. The rain continued for days as our two main characters rested inside, just listening to the gentle sound of the pouring rain. Their moods began to change. With the rain making everything so gloomy, they started to focus on themselves. They learned to appreciate themselves, their movements, their unique skin, the love within their souls. No longer did it seem like they were in a hurry. They were simply in tune with themselves, focusing on the present more than the past or future. They started to go deep down inside themselves. It was calm and peaceful as it continued to rain for many weeks. No mix of words, memories, or confusion would bring them out of the state they are in.

If you remember, at the beginning of the story, there was a soft sound in the air, a sound that they could almost see. This was before they met each other, when there was still no sun, plants, or people on the planet.

They now began to hear those soft sounds in the air again. This sound would give a person the same experience as hearing the most beautiful piece of music ever composed. It would calm a person and make one feel as gentle and soft as the day he was born. It was the feeling of one getting born again.

This experience brought them to a complete state of reflection, thinking about the day they evolved from the planet. Whoever thought the power of rain can do so much to a person's state of mind? It gets dark and gloomy when it rains for long periods. But with the power of gentle sounds of music, anyone can get through those gloomy phases of life.

The rain was not making them sad. It was simply giving them a new experience. They were being exposed to so much exotic sounds with visuals to go along with it. It was an experience, a wonderful mix of love, darkness, and peace.

All of us have a great experience in our lives at one time or another. It could be seeing a shooting star when you were a child or your first job as a young adult. It is something that changes a part of you for the better.

"But this rain though," one of them whispered to the other, "it seems to be endless."

"Do not be concerned," replied the other. "The rain will stop. Let us just relax and let the glow of the pyramid open up our chakras and add energy to our hearts."

"Yes, let us keep resting."

As the planet felt the soothing rain, "the gift" rejuvenated. The people spent time in their homes either alone or with their families. Everyone was in tune with themselves. Some were making art to express their feelings and emotions. Some got some sleep to take away the tired thoughts in their minds.

The rain seemed to slow the aliens down. Many of them have been building the pyramid for so long, they never took time to rest. Others were spending most of their days outside, socializing. And our two favorite friends had accomplished so much during their lives without slowing down. The continuous rain was like a doctor giving their patient a light sedative to relax from an overly exciting experience. Everybody needed to slow down, and the rain was doing just that for them.

It was slowing down their thoughts, making them able to focus. Slowly, every alien on the planet drifted into a deep state of meditation. Then they drifted on to dreamland as they gently fell asleep.

The people dreamed of the same thing, as if they were all in the same dream together. The soft sounds flowed through their ears and went deep within their hearts.

Together, they dreamed of the Green Fairy. The Green Fairy was their guide during REM sleep. It showed them new worlds and brought them new experiences. She was brought into their dreams from a faraway land full of other fairies. The connection she had with them was similar to the way we picture aliens today. When we talk about aliens, we usually think of green skin with oddly-shaped heads and a skinny body (though this is not really what they look like). The Green Fairy is a guide from the human mind to the realm of the aliens.

She looked almost human with fairy wings and, of course, had green skin. We should not underestimate our imagination. We picture aliens with green skin, and the Green Fairy connects us to the intelligent mind of the aliens.

And when the Green Fairy gently blew on their faces, our two favorite people woke up.

To them, it seemed like an infinite amount of years had passed. It was no longer raining. They got up and blew out the candles. The torches outside had went out because of the rain.

"What was that all about?" one of them asked. "It seems like we were in a deep trance for a long time."

"What a trip. That was amazing."

And on they went with their lives. They lived out the rest of their days as if each day was their last.

They learned so much from their experience with the Green Fairy in their dream. They knew it was a link to something that existed out there in the depth of space, somewhere beyond their galaxy and away from all their success. Our ancient ancestors perhaps dreamed of the Green Fairy and were somehow in tune with the aliens during the time of our story. This makes me think of the strong one and his beliefs. It also makes me think of the meditator, who thought more like a scientist. Together, they viewed their time during the rain as one incredible truth.

For the next few days, they stayed inside, writing, creating music, and passing the time. The galaxy was at peace. And these two were the center of it all.

They continued to stay inside for a couple of weeks. They made small fires to keep the house warm and cozy, stayed clean and took care of themselves, did stretches in the morning to keep their bodies active. They lived in harmony with each other. Slowly, they started decorating their home with paintings and chandeliers, making music to add peace to their home. They kept each other company by talking about the memories they shared, such as when they first met. They laughed about the time when they teleported for the first time to the moon and there was nothing there but dust. And they recalled the time they traveled to the nearest planet that had a pink sky and blue ground and how they met the aliens there.

What happened next was that some of the people who lived on the planet appeared to have made a special spiritual connection. Something new had arrived in their dreams during the night, and they only had one way to describe it.

The Native Americans made totem poles to express a connection to a spiritual being that accompanies them in life. Of course, different tribes have different beliefs about totem poles and what they carve or paint onto them. These poles are made from trees, and they stand tall.

Each person in a tribe has one main spirit animal that stays with them both in the physical world and the spiritual world. This one animal is basically their main spirit guide.

The aliens felt a connection with certain beings from across the universe. They began making totem poles next to the pyramid. They were tall, strong, and very thick. Painted and carved on them were pictures of different beings and animals. Their totem poles represented the beings they saw during their dreams at night. They felt like they had a permanent connection with the animals and people that they were dreaming about every night. Of course, on an alien planet, the animals do not look like the ones on Earth. Yet they were dreaming of elephants, gorillas, eagles, and many other species that exist on Earth.

The tall poles looked amazing next to the glowing pyramids.

Nights began to last longer than days. This caused the aliens' eyes to grow bigger to see better. They were adapting to their environment. They were evolving with the planet. And they were living longer with each generation.

Our two main characters came outside to see the totem poles. It made the view from their house beautiful. The bright glow from the pyramids really made the poles stand out.

Aliens from the nearby planets could see the bright enormous pyramids from where they lived. Eventually, word got around, and every person in the galaxy had seen them.

Could you imagine what could have been if these two remained enemies and never became friends in the beginning? Their friendship shows how one honest act can change the course of time. Thank goodness, these two set aside their differences at the beginning and chose friendship over greed. Think about how much we could learn from them. The power of kindness goes a long way, don't you think?

Still, they never bragged about themselves. Still, no one really knew that these two are the ones who started all this, the beginning of time, the start of the entire galaxy that now trillions of aliens inhabited. At first, only a fistful of aliens got together in a galaxy with no sun, hardly any resources, and nothing to do. Now they have reproduced so many times, and everyone was feeding off their peaceful energy and creating new worlds. The discovery of "the gift" by these two in the beginning was a true blessing, yet no one knew that. They never tried to gain recognition or praise from all their efforts.

It was in their nature to believe in themselves, and that is all they needed to live peacefully because one day, when the dust settles and life has become very exhausting, the reality that they must face is the same as that of every other living thing in the universe. Even the Green Fairy in their dreams have blessed them with eternity in their souls. For the day we face fate will only be the beginning of eternal bliss.

One day our two aliens will be covered with rocks and left to rest. Even when we are covered with earth, our souls will be preserved for the rest of time. Like the two aliens who are now lost legends in the written scrolls of time, we will have our permanent rest one day instead of just a short break from life.

Life is not so complicated. Things have a way of working out. Even our two friends had months of rain, yet it was the greatest experience of their lives. They slept with beautiful sounds in the air, then shared a dream of the Green Fairy. She became their guide and took them to places that they would never find on their own. Let's not let the rain stop us from dreaming.

Perhaps the Green Fairy will be our guide one day and take us through our journey in life. Or maybe she already has, and we haven't realized it yet.

Chapter 7

Moving on now, back to our story. Sorry for the delay, and thank you for reading thus far.

Our two favorite aliens lived their lives like villagers in a forest. It appears they preferred to be alone together despite their hospitality toward others. They are still very proud of everyone's artistic efforts with the pyramids and totem poles, but it looks like they now need to come up with something to keep them occupied. So they decided to go for a walk. They left their house and followed the river upstream, which led them up a mountain to a waterfall. They got to the top, and they could see the whole planet from there. Everyone's home looked beautiful from up there. The planet was a rich, light green color with plants and rivers running through the entire town.

People of all ages were living their lives without a care in the world. As they watched from above, they became interested in their neighbors. Perhaps they could make a few friends and have them over to listen to some music, just people to help pass the time and bring excitement into their lives.

So they made their way back down the mountain. Their neighbors were outside, most of them talking with one another. They became friends with many people in the town. Many of the neighbors invited them in their houses and made them feel at home.

Luckily enough, our friends' house was large. Most of the neighborhood came over that night to participate in music. They sang and played songs as the sun set. All through the night, the neighbors gathered around the house and sang their hearts out to the sounds of folk and blues.

It was a wonderful gathering. They never had so much fun. They had new friends, great music, and many new days to look forward to.

The dawn came. The Green Fairy woke them up by gently blowing in their faces. It was a beautiful sunrise. They began to wonder about what was going on in the rest of the galaxy. It has been so long since they even thought of visiting other planets. In their entire lifetime, they had only visited a few. The magic of "the gift" was now a part of their souls and was always running through their veins. They no longer needed to get some to use it. They could now teleport without gathering large amounts of "the gift" because it was already a part of them.

"Let's go there."

And there they were, on another planet light years away. This new planet was made of what looked like white marble, shiny, as if it were always being wiped down and cleaned. The rocks and plants there looked like they were made of mirrors. It was like a natural temple made of expensive materials. But it had only sentimental value because money does not exist anywhere in the galaxy. The aliens they found there were unlike any they have ever seen. They had clear skin, which made their vertebrae visible. Their personalities were very pleasant, yet they were not as peaceful and slow-moving like everyone else. They behaved like New Yorkers, always in a hurry and moving around a lot. Although they were very friendly people, they were not very peaceful.

"I wonder how they live."

"Let's go say hi."

After many days of spending time exploring, finding new beings and planets, our two main characters went home from a long vacation.

The neighbors missed them and welcomed them home with a warm smile. "There is no place like home," they thought. As usual, their home was full of paint, empty canvases, and old paintbrushes that have been used for legendary pieces of art.

"Let's paint that first planet we saw on our trip."

"Yeah, let's do that."

And the mural began. It was an oil painting of the deep memories within in their minds. Pictures of clear-skinned beings, the shining planet with ground that was like white marble, and the mirror-like resources that grew there. In the details of the oil painting, the small crowds of people were depicted as if they were in motion.

From here onwards, the aliens decided to make a mural of every new planet they visited.

For each painting, they both signed a certificate of authenticity and marked it with a wax stamp.

Poetry became a new interest, and these two began to write while sitting by the river. As the fish went by, they wrote words in the form of poetry. In the mix of all this development, space travel, and artistic ability, our intelligent friends thought up more words to put together than any poet in the history of the world.

Their poems ended up engraved within the walls of the pyramid. One of them read,

We began this planet alone
Yet we were never alone
It took place ages ago
The people brought hope into our hearts
The world came together in separate parts

It was engraved in gold within the passageways of the pyramid, along with their other poems. There were tunnels within the pyramid that were too dark to see your way around. But when these two engraved their poetry in the walls, it brightened up the darkness. They never told anyone that it was them who lit up the way through the inside of the pyramid. It was their little secret. Another one read,

> *The water reminds me of the ancient craters*
> *When rain filled them*
> *And now rivers cover the past*
> *Now we drink as if it were our last*

Every night they went inside the pyramid and wrote new poetry on the walls. And every night before anyone woke up, the Green Fairy lit up their torches with green flame to help them make their way back to the house.

So much art ran through the thoughts of our aliens. So much talent was transformed into the form of poetry, music, and painting. With every new planet they discovered, a new painting was made in its likeness.

New stories were being made in the form of novels and distributed among the town. These stories contained secret messages to give a little magic to the reader.

Sometimes they would tear pages from their notebook and gently toss them into the river as it flowed downstream. The clear water would take the pages along the passing rocks. The fish would begin to glow as they guided the torn pages of beautifully written poetry. Down the river, the pages would go and eventually be dissolved in the clear water, never to be recovered, as if it were never written to begin with.

Never did they seek glory for being such legends. Our two main characters never asked for much in return for their actions. Life would eventually come to a permanent halt, and honesty would carry their thoughts into the eternal abyss of nothingness within the deep reaches of space.

Time has been passing slowly. Old age is still a great distance away. The moon shines brighter every night. Life has reached a point with many experiences to look back at.

The strong one explains more about belief and truth as the meditator listens. It has been a long life full of dreams and shooting stars. The meditator learns about family and the reason behind it. They see their neighbors with children and other loved ones. But our two aliens evolved from the planet, so they never had a family. The strong one explains that family is most important. Family comes before any other thing in life. Family is about love and sharing. Kindness, along with generosity and honesty, is especially important when it comes to family.

The meditator loved learning from his friend. "I believe in most things that you talk about, about the importance of people putting value into their relationship with the ones they care about." He waited for a response from the strong one.

"The universe is full of answers. And only the right answers exist, as long as we believe in peace, love, and happiness."

"Does believing in truth make life more enjoyable?"

"Yes, enjoyment is one of life's most precious gifts. Having belief can be rewarding."

They spent a lot of their time sitting by the river, just bonding with each other, watching each other's movements and learning from each other. Their personalities matched so well. They were so independent, yet they relied so much upon each other.

Time passed. Reflecting upon the past, the aliens continued forward in life. The aliens knew one important fact: The actions of the past determine the outcome of the future.

But should our honest beings think so much about their decisions? They were forced to make one big decision at the beginning that led them to where they are now. Will they be forced to make a life-changing decision again in the future? Or will that first one change the course of time without additional effort? We are yet to find out.

Being older, they now felt more comfortable in their bodies. How long does a newly-evolved species of aliens live? The people around them had about forty to ninety years on them. But they were one of a kind, definitely not your average alien.

The world around them was growing as well and quite rapidly. The trees were almost twenty feet high and covered with vines. Mostly bright green plants and clear rivers covered everything. With everything growing so quickly, the planet looked as if it had been evolving for a million years.

Looking into the sky, the planets looked more colorful than they ever had before. The multicolored stars were brighter. And the sun still shined a nice golden yellow.

The pyramid continued to glow bright orange. From the home of our two friends, they could only see the top of it.

The totem poles stood tall and were also visible from the house.

People lived their lives peacefully and never bothered one another. Young aliens built houses within the forest. More streams would begin to flow through the land. At night, everybody would light torches outside their homes. Life has reached its peak. They could never be happier.

Chapter 8

A vast void of consciousness surrounded the galaxy. There was a blackhole awfully close to the alien civilization. It now seems as though the group of planets and stars were not meant to last. As you know, a black hole pulls in anything it gets close to. The universe has several of them. Black holes exist in space and leave no trace of anything that is pulled into it. This civilization was not meant to last. Our main characters knew that this was all temporary. They knew that nature let them choose their fate, and that they were subject to temporary existence. Maybe the two who started alien civilization as we know it did not want the credit for their accomplishments to go to other people. They were at peace.

It gave the aliens peace of mind knowing that they began life from nothing, and when they pass, they will take it all with them. And the rest that lived within their galaxy would also leave in peace.

The strong one and the meditator have now reached old age. The skin under their eyes began to sag. The backs of their arms were also drooping. They are now old aliens and were ready to live out the last few years of their life.

Will the black hole take them to another part of the galaxy? Or maybe even to another dimension? Or will that finally be the day they rest? The dust from the moon may help them find privacy, like they had in the beginning. Life is funny like that sometimes. It is as if we want to go back to what we had as children and after that, to a regular life without contact with another person.

The efforts the aliens gave seem to be from a decision that they never wanted to make. Of course, with their intelligence, they made the right decision. And after that first decision, more good ones followed.

Belief, peace, and honesty were only memories of the past. These two are old now and are only looking forward to change. Maybe this black hole was no more than just a simple wormhole that would take them to another point in time. If we can find a wormhole in space, we could use it to travel through time. Let's say we want to see the building of our Giza Pyramids in Egypt or the future of human civilization. Wormholes in space make time travel possible. Maybe one day we will find one.

Looking up, both the strong one and the meditator could see the black hole slowly sucking in the stars one by one. It moved slowly. For years, it pulled in the distant planets as the two aliens lived their lives.

At this point, they were the closest friends than they had ever been. Saying goodbye to a friend who is very near and dear to you is as dreadful as it is pleasant.

Will you, as the reader, carry on their names after the story is over? Or do their lives matter only within the pages of time?

If we keep the aliens alive in our hearts, we can change history, and life will continue for them. This leads to a choice.

As I said at the beginning, all life revolves around choice. We can choose to let our two favorite aliens live on within our hearts. It does not have to end on the last page. So what will you choose for the strong one and the meditator?

It goes a little something like this.

As the years continued to pass, the aliens moved slower. Looking up at the sun each day, they grew tired. There was not much left of the solar system now. The black hole had pretty much sucked in everything. Nothing but the sun and the moon was left for them. They were too tired to carry on.

The first place they traveled to when they first met was the moon. Of course, the planet had several moons, but the closest one was most convenient. Knowing that this is a time of saying goodbye, they traveled to that same moon. Just moments after they arrived, the strong one slowly collapsed and fell forward onto the dusty moon. The meditator looked over and saw that his lifelong friend, with whom he had lived his entire life, had passed on.

He covered the strong one with limestone-like rocks. Slowly, the meditator then began to lay down next to his best friend. Laying on his side and looking at the rocks covering the strong one, he closed his eyes and passed on.

These two lived lives that we as humans can only dream of. Now they lay to rest. Their bodies now turn to dust, blended and lost with the dust of the moon, never to be remembered. Our two aliens—our charming, loving, and much-loved favorite people—can be brought to life within our dreams, our hearts, and our wishes.

In conclusion, if you feel like a heavy burden is slowing you down in life, like you are carrying a large heavy stone on our back every day, just stop and ask a friend, "Will you help me carry the stone?"